Fairy Realm

BOOK 6

The Unicorn

ALSO BY EMILY RODDA

FairyRealm

The unicorn

book 6

EMILY RODDA

ILLUSTRATIONS BY RAOUL VITALE

HARPERCOLLINS*PUBLISHERS*

www.harperchildrens.com

Library of Congress Cataloging-in-Publication Data
Rodda, Emily.
   The unicorn / Emily Rodda.
      p.   cm. — (Fairy realm ; bk. 6)
   Originally published under the name Mary-Anne Dickinson as the
Storytelling Charms Series, 1995.
   Previously published: Sydney, N.S.W. : ABC Books, 2001.
   Summary: When wicked Queen Valda of the Outlands threatens both
the Fairy Realm and the human world, Jessie seeks the help of the uni-
.corns.
   ISBN 0-06-009598-9 — ISBN 0-06-009599-7 (lib. bdg.)
   [1. Magic—Fiction. 2. Unicorns—Fiction. 3. Fairies—Fiction.] I. Title.
PZ7.R5996Un 2004   2003051059
[Fic]—dc22   .   CIP
                                                                    AC

Typography by Karin Paprocki
1 2 3 4 5 6 7 8 9 10
❖
First American Edition
Previously published by ABC Books for the
AUSTRALIAN BROADCASTING CORPORATION
GPO Box 9994 Sydney NSW 2001
*Originally published under the name
Mary-Anne Dickinson as the Storytelling Charms Series 1995*

CONTENTS

CHAPTER ONE

Early one Morning

J essie woke just before dawn. She wasn't sure what had woken her. She sat up in bed and shivered. It was cold. Very cold. And she felt uneasy—as though something was wrong.

She listened, but Blue Moon was silent. There wasn't a sound anywhere in the old house. Everything was dark and still. She shivered again. The breeze coming through her bedroom window was icy.

"There's snow about," Granny had said the night before, as Jessie's mother, Rosemary, added a log to the crackling fire in the living room. "I'd say there'll be a fall tonight or tomorrow. Just in time for the Festival."

Remembering this, Jessie turned quickly to look out into the garden. It was still dark but she could see that there was no snow outside. Just frost, white and hard, icing the grass.

Maybe it'll snow later, thought Jessie. Oh, I hope it does.

She lay down again and cuddled deep under her quilt. It was Saturday, the day of the Winter Festival. This afternoon she was singing with the school choir at a concert in the town hall. Afterward there would be a barbecue and fireworks and dancing in the park.

Jessie knew it was going to be a tiring day. She should get some more sleep. But somehow she didn't feel like sleeping at all. That strange fearful feeling was still with her. Even the thought of snow hadn't driven it away.

Jessie closed her eyes and lay still, trying to let her mind drift. She used all the ways she knew to make herself slip back into sleep.

She counted slowly to a hundred. Then she

tried to think of things that made her feel happy and peaceful. She thought of her mother, and Granny, and Granny's big ginger cat, Flynn, all fast asleep in their beds. And, of course, she thought of the magical world of the Realm.

No one but Jessie and her grandmother knew about the invisible Door at the bottom of the Blue Moon garden. No one else knew about the enchanting fairy world beyond. Jessie had discovered them both by accident. But of course Granny had known about them all her life.

Snuggled under the covers, her eyes tightly closed, Jessie smiled. It was still so amazing to think that her own grandmother had been born in the Realm. That she was its rightful Queen, but had left it, long ago, to marry Robert Belairs, the human man she loved.

Robert had lived at Blue Moon. He'd discovered the secret Door. During his life he'd become famous for his wonderful paintings of the Realm.

Of course, everyone thought Robert Belairs had just imagined these magical fairy scenes that appeared in so many books, and hung in art galleries all over the world. But Jessie knew her grandfather had painted things he'd really seen. Fairies and elves. Mermaids and unicorns and miniature horses. Gnomes, pixies, and dwarfs. And so much more.

Jessie thought about all the extraordinary things she herself had seen and done since she had found the secret Door. She thought about all her Realm friends, especially Maybelle the miniature horse, Giff the elf, and Patrice, the palace housekeeper.

On the table beside her bed lay Jessie's charm bracelet. Every charm had been given to her by the Folk of the Realm, to remind her of her Realm adventures. As if she could ever forget. How could anyone forget such magical, exciting times?

Jessie knew she was very lucky to have found the Realm. And she was very lucky to have such a special grandmother.

Her thoughts drifted on. What would her friends think, if they knew? To them, Granny was just Mrs. Jessica Belairs of Blue Moon. Jessie's grandmother. Rosemary's mother. A widow now, since Jessie's grandfather had died. An old lady with sparkling green eyes, white hair, and a soft, laughing voice.

They didn't know how special she was. But everyone loved her. Except, of course . . .

Jessie turned over restlessly. She'd started thinking of something that *didn't* make her happy. The problem of the next-door neighbors—the Bins family.

Most people thought Granny was unusual, because she talked to her cat, and enjoyed walking in the rain, and things like that. But they liked her just the way she was.

The Bins family didn't. Mr. and Mrs. Bins, and their daughter, Irena, thought Granny was crazy. They never stopped making jokes about her and causing trouble. And now that Mr. Bins was town mayor, he was ruder and more unpleasant than ever. He seemed to think he was so important that he could say and do anything he wanted to.

At school Irena was always giggling and whispering to her friends about mad old Mrs. Belairs, and the latest loopy thing she'd done.

Jessie's own friends told her not to take any notice. But she couldn't help it. And just lately everything had become even worse. Because of Grey Prince.

Grey Prince was Irena's pony. She asked and asked her parents for a horse, and when they finally bought the pretty gray pony for her, she was very pleased and proud. She talked about him all the time, brought all her friends to see him, and rode him every day.

But after a while she became bored with him. She said grooming and feeding him was a lot of trouble and took too much of her time. She started begging her parents for a new bike. And once she had that, she stopped riding Grey Prince every day. She went out on her bike with her friends instead.

As the months went by, Irena spent less and less time with Grey Prince. Every day he stood, lonely, in his paddock at the bottom of the Bins' garden. His shiny coat grew dull and rough. His mane and tail were tangled with prickles and burrs.

When, once in a while, Irena did decide to ride him, he'd rear and back away, so it was hard for her to put the saddle on his back. Then she'd hit him with her riding crop, and shout at him, before stomping away, grumbling angrily.

"Look at that poor animal down there," Granny would say fiercely, looking over the fence from the back door of Blue Moon. "It's a disgrace! He needs grooming. He needs exercise. He's lonely. He's miserable!"

Then she would go inside and get a carrot or two, and take them down to Grey Prince, pushing through the bushes that grew thickly beside the fence between Blue Moon and the Bins' house.

The fence made one side of Grey Prince's paddock. Granny would lean over it, holding out the carrots and calling gently to the pony till he came over to her and ate.

"Mum, the Bins won't like you making friends with that horse." Rosemary sighed. "You should stay away from him. You know what they're like."

"Someone's got to keep him company, Rosemary," Granny said. "And why should the Bins object, anyway? They don't care about Grey Prince."

"No," Rosemary answered. "But if they find out you're making a fuss of him they'll get angry. You wait and see."

Granny smiled. "You worry too much, darling," she said. "Never mind. All will be well."

Rosemary shook her head and raised her eyebrows at Jessie. You could tell that she wasn't so sure.

It wasn't very long before Granny was visiting Grey Prince a few times every day. Sometimes she took him a carrot or a bunch of sweet grass; sometimes she just stood talking to him, stroking his nose, or pulling prickles from his mane to make him more comfortable.

Jessie went with her after school most days. Soon a little track had been worn between the bushes by the fence in that part of the Blue Moon garden.

Grey Prince liked the visits. He seemed to look forward to them. When he heard Granny's voice he trotted up to put his head over the fence, snuffling softly. And when it was time for her to leave he looked sad.

"I'll come back soon," Granny would promise him. And she always kept her word.

One day, at the beginning of winter, Mr. Bins came down to toss a bundle of hay into the paddock, and saw Grey Prince with Granny and Jessie by the side fence.

"Hey!" he shouted angrily. "Mrs. Belairs! What are you doing there, may I ask?"

Jessie jumped nervously, but Granny only smiled. "I'm just visiting Grey Prince, Mr. Bins," she called.

Mr. Bins went red in the face and moved closer. "Well, I'll thank you to leave him alone," he said. "He's skittish enough as it is, without you upsetting him."

"He's skittish because he needs exercise," said Granny. "He stands here day after day with no one to talk to. He's bored, Mr. Bins. He's unhappy. And he's getting cold. He needs a shelter for the winter. Or a blanket, at least. You should do something about it."

"You mind your own business," snapped Mr. Bins. "And from now on, keep away from that fence or I'll have the law onto you."

Granny lifted her chin. Her green eyes flashed. "I will go wherever I like in my own garden, Mr. Bins," she said firmly. "And if Grey Prince wants to chat with me over the fence, he can."

Grey Prince opened his mouth and snickered. You'd almost think he'd understood every word she'd said and was agreeing with her.

Uh-oh, thought Jessie, watching Mr. Bins' face deepen to a strange purple color. Here's trouble.

And she was right. After that day, the war between Granny and the Bins family grew much worse.

Irena wouldn't speak to Jessie at school. She told her friends that Jessie's crazy grandmother had been messing around with Grey Prince, feeding him strange things and upsetting him. Also that Granny had been very rude to her father, the mayor. She said her father was going to see a lawyer about it.

When Jessie told Granny about that, Granny laughed. "I haven't done anything wrong, Jessie," she said. "Irena's just making up stories to make herself look important."

But then some men came and put up a new side fence on Grey Prince's paddock. A fence that stopped him coming and putting his head over into the Blue Moon garden. It made his paddock smaller. And of course Granny couldn't bring him carrots or stroke his nose anymore.

Granny was very angry, and very sad. So was Jessie. They could see Grey Prince, cold and lonely in his paddock, but they couldn't talk to him or touch him. And since then Grey Prince had become more and more miserable every day.

CHAPTER TWO

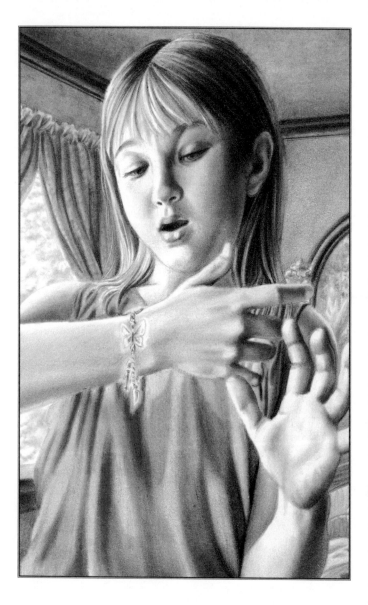

"something's wrong!"

J essie pulled the quilt over her head to try to shut out the picture of Grey Prince. She knew there was nothing she could do to help him. "Don't think about it," she told herself. "You're supposed to be thinking of happy things."

She tossed and turned for a few more minutes and finally sat up in bed again. There was no way she could go back to sleep. The feeling that something was wrong was niggling away at her, growing stronger and stronger.

Was it Grey Prince? No. The feeling had begun before Jessie had even started thinking about him.

Was it the concert this afternoon? No, of course not. There was no reason to feel nervous about that.

Jessie slipped out of bed and put on her dressing gown and slippers. The sky outside her window had started to lighten. Dawn was breaking.

Somehow Jessie knew that this wasn't going to be an ordinary day. Something was going to happen. And she wanted to be ready when it did.

On impulse, she picked up her charm bracelet and began to fasten it around her wrist. As she did, her fingers tingled. She gasped. And at once she knew.

Whatever was wrong, it was something to do with the Realm. And it was serious.

Hurrying now, she left her room and padded down the hallway. To her surprise she saw that a light was on in the kitchen. She peeped in. There was Granny, fully dressed, sitting at the table drinking tea. Flynn was at her feet. So she, too, had woken early.

"Granny," whispered Jessie.

Granny looked up, and their eyes met.

"Something's wrong!" Jessie said.

Her grandmother nodded. "You felt it, too," she said. "I wondered if you would. I've been sitting here thinking that you and I had better go to the Realm and see what the trouble is. If we leave straight after breakfast we'll have plenty of time for a quick visit before we have to go to the concert."

"Yes," Jessie agreed. She tried to sound grown-up and casual, but she didn't feel it. She knew that her grandmother wouldn't be planning to go to the Realm unless she thought the problem was very serious. Granny's sister, Helena, ruled as Queen now. Granny usually liked to leave Helena to manage things her own way, without interfering.

Jessie went to the sink to get herself a glass of water. As always, when she knew she would be going to the Realm, her heart was fluttering with excitement. But as she looked out at the chilly, cloudy morning, she realized that she was afraid, too.

She turned to look at Granny. Her grandmother's head was bent. She was staring at her cup on the table, deep in thought. She looked worried—and confused.

15

"I can't understand it, Jessie," she murmured. "This feeling—it's so strange. I know the trouble's in the Realm. But somehow it seems closer than that. It seems—as though it's here, as well."

"I know," whispered Jessie. "But how can it be? It's scary."

Flynn meowed loudly.

"Never mind," said Granny, stroking his neck, and speaking as much to him as to Jessie. "We'll find out soon enough. And whatever it is, we'll deal with it."

Her voice sounded as calm as usual. But her green eyes were troubled. And beside her Flynn sat up straighter, as though he was on guard.

Granny, Rosemary, and Jessie were finishing breakfast when the phone rang.

"Who can that be?" exclaimed Granny. She jumped up, crossed the room quickly and picked up the phone.

She listened for a couple of minutes, her face growing more and more troubled. "I'll be there as soon as I can," she said finally. "Thank you."

She put down the phone and stood for a moment with her hands clasped, looking out of the window.

"Mum, what's wrong?" asked Rosemary urgently.

"That was the hospital. Hazel Bright was in a car accident early this morning," Granny said slowly. "You know she's been away? She was coming back today, in time for the Winter Festival. Must have decided to get here early, to beat the traffic. But just outside town her car ran off the road and hit a tree."

"Oh no! Is she all right?" Jessie burst out. This was terrible. Hazel Bright was Granny's dearest friend—a kind, busy woman whose house was just around the corner from Blue Moon.

"She's quite badly hurt." Granny ran a trembling hand over her forehead. "She's asking for me, the hospital said. I have to go."

She frowned. Jessie knew what she was thinking. Was this the trouble they had both felt was coming?

It couldn't be, Jessie thought. The trouble was something to do with the Realm. And Mrs. Bright might be Granny's best friend, but she was still

17

just an ordinary human, who knew nothing about Granny's fairy world.

"Mum, don't worry. I'm sure Hazel will be okay," Rosemary said gently. "Now, look, you finish your breakfast while I get dressed. Then I'll take you to the hospital."

"Oh no, Rosemary," cried Granny. "You've been working at the hospital all week. The last thing you need is to be going there again today, on your day off. I'll be fine on my own."

Rosemary grinned. "Don't be silly, Mum. Of course I'll take you. I don't want you driving when you're all upset. You'll end up wrapped around a tree just like Hazel. Come on. Nurse's orders."

Granny shook her head. The phone rang again.

"What now?" Rosemary sighed. This time she answered the phone herself.

When she put the receiver down, she turned to them and made a face.

"Looks like this is a morning for accidents," she said. "I'll be taking you to the hospital whether you like it or not, Mum. Diana Trevini slipped and fell in the hospital car park, on her way to work.

18

She's sprained her ankle. They need me to go in and work today in her place. Can you believe it?"

She turned to Jessie. "Darling, I'm sorry," she said. "I had to say I'd help them out. I can't leave the hospital short of nurses. But the concert . . . Now I can't go, and Granny mightn't be able to go either."

"Oh, the concert doesn't matter at all," said Jessie. "Really, Mum. It's not important. I'm just in the choir. At the back." She half grinned and tried to joke. "It's a shame you have to work. But don't forget, if you miss the concert, you miss Mr. Bins' long, boring speech, too. That's one good thing."

Her mother patted her cheek and smiled back at her. "You'd better go over to Sal's for the day, darling. Then you can go to the concert together. I'll ring Sal's mother and—"

"Mum, I'd rather stay here," Jessie broke in quickly, glancing at Granny. "There are . . . things I want to do this morning. I can walk to the town hall when it's time to go. No problem."

Rosemary looked at her doubtfully for a moment. Then she glanced at her watch and came

19

to a quick decision. "All right," she said, turning away and making for her bedroom to get dressed. "But you be good and take care, Jessie. And ring me at the hospital if you need me."

"I will," said Jessie. "But everything will be fine." *I hope*, she added to herself, looking into her grandmother's worried eyes as Rosemary hurried away.

"Jessie," Granny began. "Are you sure you should—"

Jessie took her hand. The charm bracelet jingled on her wrist. "I'm sure, Granny," she said. "Of course I'm sure. You don't have to worry about me. You know I've been to the Realm by myself lots of times."

Granny shook her head. "This is different," she said. "Oh, I wish I could go with you, Jessie. But I have to go to Hazel. She needs me."

"Of course she does," said Jessie. "And of course you have to go to her."

Granny frowned. "The trouble is, I think the Realm needs me, too," she went on. "It's terrible to have to turn my back on it."

"Well, you're not turning your back on it, are

20

you?" said Jessie firmly. "You're sending me in your place. I'll go to the Realm and find out what's going on. And if—if there's any news, I'll ring you at the hospital and tell you. All right?"

"All right." At last Granny managed a small smile. Again she looked out of the window at the sky. She shivered. "My word, it looks cold out there," she said. "It's definitely going to snow."

She stood on her toes and looked down through the trees to the end of the Bins' garden. Her face was pale and anxious. Jessie knew she was thinking of Grey Prince, cold and alone in his paddock, with snow on the way.

Granny usually didn't worry about anything. But now she had three things to worry about. Hazel Bright, Grey Prince—and the Realm.

Well, Jessie couldn't do anything about the first two things, but she could do something about the third. And she was going to do it. As soon as she could. As soon as her mother and grandmother left for the hospital, she was going to make her own journey.

Into the Realm.

CHAPTER THREE

In the Realm

It was freezing outside. The morning sun was completely hidden behind thick, heavy-looking clouds.

Jessie wrapped her jacket more tightly around her as she jogged away from the house, through the trees. She slipped through the door in the hedge that surrounded the special place she called the secret garden.

It was peaceful there, as always. Smooth green grass. Rosemary bushes, gray and sweet-smelling. Here Jessie always felt that she was in a world of her own. It was as if the hedge made walls that kept worries and problems out.

But today Jessie didn't have time to enjoy the peace and silence. She stood in the center of the small, square lawn and closed her eyes.

"Open!" she called. And at once she felt the familiar breeze rushing into her face, lifting her long red hair so that it flew around her shoulders. There was a rushing, sighing sound. Her whole body tingled.

And then—it wasn't cold anymore.

Jessie opened her eyes.

She was in the Realm. She was standing on the pebbly road. The sky above her was blue. The hedge that protected the Realm from its enemies, the wicked creatures of the Outlands, rose high and dark beside her. Golden sunshine beamed softly down. Everything was just as it always was.

But no fairies giggled among the leaves of the trees. No tiny horses nibbled grass in the clearings. And the road was empty, for as far as the eye could see.

"Where is everyone?" Jessie murmured. She pulled off her jacket and started trudging along the road toward the palace.

After a few minutes she reached the grove of tall, pale-leaved trees that she had walked through so many times in the past.

Still she had seen no one. But she knew that behind these trees was the great golden palace. There she would find Patrice, the palace housekeeper. Queen Helena, too. And maybe, if she was lucky, Giff the elf, and Maybelle.

As she moved off the road and began threading her way through the trees, she became aware of a strange sound in the distance. A dull, roaring sound, coming from the direction of the palace.

At first she didn't know what it was. And then she realized. She was hearing the roar of voices. Many, many voices. It sounded as though hundreds of people were calling out, all at once.

"What's going on?" Jessie said aloud, frowning. She started to run.

Soon she could see the golden spires of the palace rising above the treetops. The noise grew louder and louder. There was a huge crowd ahead, all right. Now she could hear singing and laughing, as well as chatter.

Well, they don't sound too worried, anyway, she thought. A wave of relief washed over her. It looked as though she and Granny had been wrong. People wouldn't sound so happy if there was a serious problem in the Realm.

She wiped her forehead with the back of her hand. She was hot. Her winter clothes were much too warm for this sunshiny day.

Just then a great cheer rose up in the distance. "Helena! Helena!" shouted hundreds of voices, big and small.

Jessie hurried through the last of the trees. The palace rose before her, gleaming in the sunlight. Queen Helena, wearing a beautiful blue dress and a golden crown, was standing at one of the long front windows on the first floor. She was smiling and waving to the crowd gathered on the grass below.

Jessie blinked at the sight. There were dwarfs, gnomes, and elves, tiny horses with ribbons and bells in their manes, finely dressed fairy Folk. And there were water sprites with pale green hair, thin little people she thought must be brownies, brightly dressed pixies, and many other creatures that Jessie had never seen before.

All of them were laughing, cheering, and waving back to their Queen, while fairies darted like a rainbow cloud of butterflies around their heads.

After a few moments Queen Helena held up her hands for silence. Everyone quieted and waited for her to speak. Jessie stood motionless in the shadow of the trees, listening as Helena's voice rang out like a sweet, high bell. She could hear the words clearly.

"I thank you for coming to this meeting, people of the Realm," said Queen Helena. "I ask you to spread the news I am about to tell you. It is important. Everyone must know of it."

The crowd was very still now. Even the tiny fairies had stopped fluttering and dancing. Queen Helena spoke on.

"I am sorry to tell you that early this morning we had word of a strange happening in the west. Our people there have become aware of a great crowd massing on the other side of the hedge. They fear that the creatures of the Outlands will try to break through there, and attack the Realm."

There was a frightened murmur from the listening crowd. Queen Helena raised her voice a little.

"I do not tell you this to make you afraid. Our magic is strong. The hedge holds as firm as ever. As far as we can tell there is still no way the Outlanders, or their leader, my cousin Valda, can break through. Valda was banished to the Outlands long ago. But she has tried to come back to the Realm before. And she is clever and determined."

"And full of anger and spite!" shouted an elf.

Queen Helena nodded sadly. "I am sorry to say that is true," she said. "Valda wants to be Queen of the Realm in my place, and—"

"Never!" called many voices.

"She wants to make us into slaves!" growled a dwarf, his hand on his sword.

"Take all our gold," bellowed a gnome.

"She will let her ogres and trolls destroy our beautiful land," sang the fairies. "Turn it into a dark, cold place like their own. With no flowers. No fresh streams. No green trees."

The miniature horses said nothing. They just

looked at one another and pawed the ground with their tiny hoofs. But Jessie knew what they were thinking, and how afraid they were. She knew that Valda wanted to round them all up and take them away in chains, to work underground in the mines of the Outlands.

Queen Helena held up her hands again. When everyone was still, she went on speaking.

"As I said, we do not believe that it is possible for the Outlanders to break down the hedge and get through to us," she said. "But, just in case, my guards and I are going, now, to the west."

"No, Queen Helena," cried many voices. "Don't go! Don't go into danger!"

Helena smiled. "Of course I must go, friends," she said. "If by any chance Valda *has* found a way of weakening the hedge, my magic will be needed to strengthen it again. But do not fear. I will be safe. My guards will protect me. And anyway, we will almost certainly find that the Outlanders are gathering for quite another reason, and that there is no danger threatening the Realm at all."

Peering through the low branches of the trees,

Jessie frowned. Helena sounded calm, but how would she feel if she knew that Jessie and Granny had been woken this morning by feelings of fear?

Whatever was happening in the west, the danger to the Realm was real. Jessie knew it.

She listened carefully as Queen Helena started speaking again, in her clear, ringing voice.

"I must say goodbye to you now, friends. I can delay my journey no longer. Keep safe and happy until I return."

She put both hands to her lips and blew the crowd a kiss. Then, with a final wave, she moved away from the window. Two guards shut it.

"Oh, isn't the Queen coming down to dance with us?" squeaked a small fairy voice in the tree high above Jessie's head.

"Of course not, you silly!" shrilled another voice. "Didn't you listen? The Queen is going to the west! With the guards! She hasn't got time for dancing."

Jessie looked up. There among the leaves she could see five tiny, fluttering figures. She smiled. Bluebell, Daisy, Violet, Rose, and Daffodil—her little flower fairy friends. They were so busy talking to each other that they hadn't seen her yet.

She opened her mouth to call them, but quickly shut it again. Once the fairies saw her, they'd pounce on her and plague her to dance with them. Especially now that Queen Helena had disappeared inside the palace.

But Jessie didn't have time for dancing today. And she didn't have time for a long argument, either. She needed to speak to Queen Helena before the Queen left on her journey. Tell her about Granny's fear, warn her that the trouble was serious. Then she had to get back to her own world, to let Granny know what was happening.

There was no time to waste.

no time to waste

J essie stepped out from the trees and hurried toward the palace as fast as she could. But many people and creatures were still milling around on the grass, and it took a long time for her to edge between them and reach the great golden doors.

"Please," she said to one of the guards standing there. "Please let me in. I need to speak to Queen Helena. Very urgently."

The guard looked doubtful.

"Please!" urged Jessie. "I have a message for her. From my grandmother, Queen Jessica."

"Jessie!" squeaked a voice from a window above her head. Jessie looked up and saw the rosy face of Patrice looking down at her in surprise.

"Beekle," Patrice called. "What are you thinking of, letting Princess Jessie stand there? Please let her in at once. I'm coming down." She turned away from the window. "Giff, Maybelle!" Jessie heard her shout. "Guess who's here?"

The guard stared at Jessie, then he nodded, unlocked the door, and stood aside. Jessie slipped past him into the palace.

The wide staircase that led to the first floor rose before her. Down the stairs, with a patter of hurrying feet, came the small, plump figure of Patrice. Behind her were Giff the elf, shrieking with excitement, and Maybelle, the miniature horse.

Patrice reached the bottom of the stairs and ran toward Jessie, her arms outstretched. Giff tried to do the same, somersaulted over the bottom step, and fell to the floor in a tangled heap. Maybelle stepped over him, snorting in disgust.

"Jessie!" Patrice exclaimed, hugging her tightly. "What are you doing here?"

"I have to see Queen Helena, Patrice." Jessie gasped. "I have something to tell her. About the troubles in the west."

Patrice looked worried. Giff, still picking himself up from the floor, clapped his hands over his mouth and fell over again.

Maybelle shook her head. The red ribbons in her mane fluttered. "Queen Helena and the guards have gone, Jessie," she said. "They left as soon as she'd finished speaking to the crowd. They were flying. We'll never catch them now."

"But we have to!" Jessie exclaimed. "Maybelle, there really *is* trouble in the west. There must be. Granny and I both woke early this morning feeling that something bad was going to happen. I have to tell Queen Helena. Warn her."

Maybelle glanced over her shoulder to see if anyone else was listening. But the doors were closed, and the big entrance hall was empty.

"Keep your voice down, Jessie," she warned. "We don't want creatures to be any more worried than they already are. Look, we'll send a flying messenger after the Queen, to tell her what you've said." She frowned. "This makes everything look very much more serious, doesn't it?"

Giff shuffled up to them, his pointed ears drooping. He took Jessie's hand.

"Queen Helena feared the worst," said Patrice grimly. "I told you, Maybelle. I know her so well. She didn't want the people to panic, so she made it sound as though she wasn't really worried. But she *was* worried. I could tell. She took almost all the guards with her, for a start. Why would she do that if she didn't really believe the news from the west?"

"I don't understand!" wailed Giff. "Valda was banished. The hedge between the Realm and the Outlands is still strong. Everyone says it is. Queen Helena promised that Valda would never, ever be able to get through it again. So how . . . ?"

"We don't *know*, Giff!" snapped Maybelle. "I've told you that a hundred times already. We don't *know* what Valda's plan is. We only wish we did."

Giff sniffed. Then, suddenly, he gave a little gasp and squeezed Jessie's hand. "Jessie can help us!" he yelped. "Jessie has helped us before. She can tell us about Valda's plan!"

He looked up at Jessie confidently, the tips of his ears glowing with excitement.

Jessie's heart sank.

"Giff, I'm sorry," she said finally. "I wish I could help. But this time I just don't know how. I don't know much about magic. When I've helped before, it's just been by using human common sense. And I don't think that's much use at the moment."

Slowly Giff's ears drooped again. "Oh," he said in a small voice.

"But what I can do," Jessie hurried on, "is go home straight away and tell Granny what's happening here. Maybe *she* can do something. She doesn't usually like to interfere. But if the Realm's in real danger . . ."

Maybelle pawed the ground. "And it is!" she huffed.

Patrice nodded violently. "It is!" she repeated. "And yes, Jessie, you're right! We should have thought of it before. If Queen Jessica will come back to the Realm, and add her magic to Queen

Helena's, maybe we can stop Valda's wickedness before it begins."

Giff began to look hopeful again.

Jessie smiled at him. "I'll go right now," she said. "And the next time you see me, Giff, I'll probably have Granny with me. So don't worry any more."

Giff nodded, and blew his nose loudly on a white-spotted green handkerchief.

"Come on, then," ordered Maybelle. "Let's stop wasting time. Patrice, you go and send a messenger off to Queen Helena. I'll go back to the Door with Jessie, and see that she gets home safely. Giff, you'd better come with us. I don't want you getting into trouble."

Usually Patrice argued when Maybelle was bossy, but not this time. She just nodded, kissed Jessie goodbye, and trotted off to find a messenger.

Jessie knew why Patrice hadn't argued. Both she and Patrice understood what lay beneath Maybelle's brave expression and bossy words. The little horse wouldn't show it, of course. But she was terribly afraid.

As soon as Patrice had gone, Maybelle, Jessie, and Giff left the palace and headed toward the grove and pale-leaved trees. Ten minutes later they were standing on the roadway outside the Door. Giff clung tightly to Jessie's hand.

Maybelle tossed her mane. "Goodbye, Jessie," she said in a gruff voice. "Bring Queen Jessica back with you as soon as you can. We'll be waiting."

Jessie bent and pressed her cheek against the tiny horse's soft white head. "Everything will be all right, Maybelle," she whispered. Then she kissed Giff's cheek. "See you soon!" she said, gently pulling her hand away from his.

She turned to face the hedge. "Open!" she called.

As the breeze rushed into her face, and the tingling feeling began, she glanced back over her shoulder. Through a golden mist she saw that Giff and Maybelle were gazing after her. Maybelle's ribbons were fluttering bravely. Giff's hand was raised in a wave. Behind them the grass was green and soft, and fairies chattered and laughed in the trees.

It's all so beautiful, thought Jessie. I love it so much. And for a moment fear gripped her heart. Then her eyes closed as she felt herself spinning away, back to Blue Moon.

When Jessie opened her eyes, all she could see for a moment was blinding white. She gasped in shock, then shuddered with cold. It was freezing!

While she had been away in the Realm, it had started snowing.

The snow was whirling around her now, falling from dark, heavy skies. Snow lay on the ground, covering the smooth grass of the secret garden in a blanket of white. The rosemary bushes were half buried. There was a hush over everything.

Jessie struggled into her jacket and pulled it tightly around her. With her eyes half shut against the snow, she ran, stumbling and slipping, out of the secret garden and through the trees to the house.

Everything looked so different! All color seemed to have disappeared. The whole of Blue Moon was black, gray, and white.

Flynn was sitting upright by the back door. He meowed loudly as Jessie reached him.

"Oh, Flynn." Jessie gasped. "There's terrible trouble in the Realm. I have to ring Granny at the hospital straight away."

Flynn rumbled in his throat. He seemed to understand exactly what she was saying. He moved away from the door as Jessie opened it, and followed her inside.

Jessie pulled off her wet shoes and ran into the kitchen. She snatched up the phone and started to dial. Halfway through she realized that something was wrong. She listened, and her stomach turned over. The phone was dead!

"A power line must have come down somewhere, Flynn," she said aloud. "The snow . . ."

Her heart pounded. What was she going to do? The hospital was right over on the other side of town. It would take her ages to walk there. Especially in the snow.

She ran to the kitchen window and looked out. Snow still fell heavily. At the bottom of the Bins' garden Grey Prince was standing miserably in his paddock. Jessie felt a pang. But she knew she couldn't think about poor Grey Prince now.

Looking at him gave her an idea, though. Mr. Bins had a mobile phone. She'd seen him with it, lots of times.

She ran to the front of the house and out the door. White yard, swirling snow, deserted street. Panting, she ran out the front gate and started toward the house next door.

She had just reached the Bins' front verandah when she heard it: Mr. Bins' voice, laughing and loud, coming from the sitting room.

"Nonsense, dear lady," he was saying. "It's a great, great pleasure to have you. I'm only sorry my wife is away from home today, but you'll meet her later, at the town hall."

There was an answering murmur.

"You'll stay with us for lunch. Irena and I insist," boomed Mr. Bins. "Someone who is going to bring so many visitors to our little town is more than welcome in my home."

Jessie looked through the window.

There was a fire burning. Mr. Bins and Irena

were sitting in chairs drawn up to the fireplace.

And in a third chair was someone else. A proud, elegant-looking woman wearing a long purple cape. She was very beautiful. Her green eyes shone. Her magnificent red hair was twisted into a heavy knot on the nape of her neck. She was smiling.

Jessie pressed her hand to her mouth to stop herself from crying out. She couldn't believe what she was seeing.

The woman was Valda!

valda

Jessie's mind raced. What was Valda doing here? It was the very last place Jessie would ever have expected to see her. And *how* had she come?

"Our little concert is this afternoon," Mr. Bins was saying. Through the window Jessie could see him rubbing his hands together, leaning forward in his chair. "The start of the Winter Festival, you know. As mayor I am, of course, making a speech. I can introduce you to our little community then."

"Wonderful," purred Valda. "I just *knew* it was best to come and see you first, Mr. Bins. Before anyone else. The most important man in town. The one who would best understand my idea."

Mr. Bins puffed out his chest proudly.

Don't be fooled by her, Mr. Bins, Jessie thought fiercely. Somehow she's trying to trick you. She's trying to get something she wants.

But what *did* Valda want? Why was she wasting time here, in the Bins' sitting room, instead of leading her hideous army of ogres and trolls in the Outlands of the Realm?

"Such a *pretty* little town," Valda said, smiling. "I know my tour parties will love it. And, of course, the tourists will want to buy things here. Food and gifts, and so on. They will bring a lot of money to the town, Mr. Bins. And, as mayor, you know how important that is."

"Oh yes," said Mr. Bins. He rubbed his hands together again.

"I do hope I will be able to see my poor old cousin Jessica before I leave," Valda went on, looking down at her long red fingernails. "She doesn't appear to be home at present."

Jessie jumped. Valda was talking about Granny!

46

Mr. Bins looked slightly uncomfortable for the first time. He glanced at his daughter. Jessie saw Irena raise her eyebrows and snigger.

"I can't think why Mrs. Belairs would be out on a day like this," Mr. Bins said after a moment. "And wherever she is, she may have trouble getting back to Blue Moon—at least until the snow melts."

He cleared his throat. "We don't know her very well, Miss Outlander," he added. "She is—ah—an unusual woman."

Valda laughed, long and low. She leaned forward. "Poor old Jessica has always been rather odd," she murmured. "And just between us, it's not actually *her* I want to see. But I have always loved her dear house. Such a beautiful garden! I would adore to see over it again. Especially now, in the snow."

"Ah!" Mr. Bins nodded knowingly. "Well, I'm sure we can arrange that, Miss Outlander. I'm sure Mrs. Belairs couldn't object if you were to have a little wander in her garden—even while she was out. After all, you *are* her cousin."

"I could take you round *our* garden, if you like," Irena said loudly. "It's *just* as nice as the Blue Moon garden. And I have a horse, and everything."

"How lovely," cooed Valda, fixing her with those shining green eyes. "Well, perhaps a little later, Irena dear. As for the Blue Moon garden, I'm sure Jessica's granddaughter, Jessie, could show it to me. I have a feeling she, at least, will be home soon."

Jessie jumped. Her heart pounded. It was terrifying to hear Valda talking about her like this.

And at that very moment, Valda raised her head and looked straight at her through the window.

Terrified, frozen to the spot, Jessie saw the red lips curve in a triumphant smile.

"Well, well," Valda said, pointing. "It seems I was right. Here's Jessie now. She must have come to pay you a visit. Isn't that a lucky chance?"

Mr. Bins and Irena turned in their chairs to look. They frowned at Jessie through the window.

Valda stood up. "I must have a little chat with her," she said.

"Of course, of course," mumbled Mr. Bins. He clambered out of his chair and left the room to open the door, with Valda close behind him.

Jessie stood on the verandah, not knowing what to do. The door swung open. Mr. Bins' face glared out at her.

"Your grandmother's cousin is here, Jessie," he said coldly. "We are having a business discussion."

Valda stepped out from behind him. "How nice to see you again, Jessie," she purred, fixing Jessie with her piercing eyes. "I have been looking forward to it."

Jessie found her voice. "What are you doing here?" she whispered.

Valda laughed. A most unpleasant laugh. "Now, is that any way to greet a relative, Jessie?" she asked. "After all the trouble I've taken to get here, too?"

Jessie said nothing.

"Mind your manners, Jessie," said Mr. Bins severely. "Miss Outlander would like you to take her over to the Blue Moon garden."

Jessie shook her head. She cleared her throat.

"My grandmother and my mother are out," she managed to say. "I'm not allowed to have anyone in the house while they're gone."

Valda smiled. "Of course," she said. "But after all, it's only the garden I want to see. And I *am* your grandmother's cousin, Jessie. Isn't that so?"

"Yes," murmured Jessie. Her head was whirling. Behind Valda, Mr. Bins was scowling furiously. For sure he thought she was being very stupid and rude.

He didn't know about the Realm. Or who the woman calling herself Valda Outlander really was. He'd never believe Jessie if she told him. They'd think she was lying, or crazy.

"You had better do as I ask, Jessie," said Valda. She was still smiling, but Jessie could see the angry warning in her eyes. "I have a feeling your grandmother and mother won't be back today. It's very unfortunate. Such a lot of accidents, all at once."

Jessie's breath caught in her throat. She realized what Valda was telling her. Her mother, and Granny, had been got out of the way on purpose.

Hazel Bright's car accident, Diana Trevini's fall—both of those things were Valda's doing.

All along Valda had been planning for this. To get Jessie alone, and helpless.

But why? Why?

"Well?" cooed Valda. "What do you think? Will you take me for a walk in your beautiful garden?"

Jessie couldn't say anything. But stubbornly she shook her head.

"Jessie, really!" exploded Mr. Bins.

Valda turned to him. "Never mind, Mr. Bins," she said. "I've taken Jessie by surprise. I'm sure she'll change her mind once she thinks about it."

She turned back to Jessie and looked straight into her eyes. "I really hope you will, Jessie. Before it's time for me to go to the concert this afternoon." She paused. "Still, if you don't, I'll have to find a way to cheer myself up," she went on. "Won't I?"

Her face brightened. "I know. All your little school friends are singing in the choir at the concert, aren't they? So sweet. I have a group of friends just nearby. I could give them a call. We could make a party of it. Go to the concert together. I'm sure my friends would *love* to meet the choir."

She reached out and touched Jessie's shoulder. Her hand felt like ice. Jessie could feel the aching cold right through her clothes. "You just think about it, Jessie," she said. Her fingers tightened.

Terrified, Jessie tore herself away. "No!" she shouted. She turned and ran. Away from the house, down the front path, and into the street. Snowflakes whirled around her, blinding her. She slipped and fell.

"Jessie!" roared Mr. Bins in fury. "Stop! Come back here!"

"Oh, let her go, Mr. Bins," Jessie heard Valda cry. "I'll go to see her soon. When she's done some thinking. She'll do as I ask—in the end."

Jessie picked herself up and stumbled on. She heard Valda's high, mocking laughter floating after her as she flung open the Blue Moon gate and darted through it.

She ran to the back of the house, floundering in

the snow that covered the path. Flynn was there, by the back door, keeping guard.

"Flynn!" Jessie shouted. "Get Granny! I need her. And be careful! Valda!"

Flynn stared at her with wide eyes. She didn't know if he could understand her. She didn't know what he could do to help, even if he did understand. All she knew was that she had to get to the one place where Valda couldn't follow. The one place where she would be safe.

Panting and crying, she ran through the trees to the secret garden.

She had to get to the Realm.

what to do?

"Oh, she's dead, she's dead. I know she is!"

Dimly, Jessie heard a voice wailing and sobbing. Giff, she thought slowly. She felt someone stroking her forehead, and warm sun on her face. She tried to open her eyes, but couldn't.

"Don't be ridiculous, Giff. She's not dead, or anything like it," snapped another voice. "She's fainted, that's all. Move away from her. Give her room to breathe. She's waking up."

At last Jessie managed to lift her heavy eyelids. She saw Giff's face, and Maybelle's. And, behind their heads, darting flashes of color. Fairies. Silent, for once, and watching her anxiously.

"I'm all right," she managed to say.

"All *right*?" snapped Maybelle, covering up her worry, as usual, by pretending to be cross. "What do you mean, all right? You came crashing through the Door and fainted. You were freezing. You're soaking wet. What in the Realm happened to you?"

She didn't ask why Jessie hadn't brought Granny with her. She knew that something shocking had happened to stop her doing as she'd promised. She waited for Jessie to explain.

"It's snowing," whispered Jessie. "So cold. And . . ."

Her voice trailed off. She looked up at the anxious, fluttering fairies. She didn't want to tell Maybelle about Valda while the fairies were there. They would be terribly frightened and would rush around telling everyone about it. Jessie knew it was important to work a few things out before that happened.

Luckily Maybelle understood. "Up you get,"

she said briskly. "I'm taking you to the palace. You need a rest and a warm drink. Come on, Giff."

Giff helped Jessie to her feet and together the friends moved slowly away. Jessie still felt weak and dizzy, and her teeth were chattering, despite the warm sun, but she managed to wave to the fairies and smile. They waved sadly back. They could see that this wasn't a good time for dancing.

Giff was full of questions, but Maybelle wouldn't let Jessie say another word until they were safely inside Patrice's cozy little kitchen at the palace.

Patrice, exclaiming and wondering, rushed around making hot chocolate, and finding Jessie a dressing gown to put on while her clothes dried.

Only when Maybelle saw Jessie sitting comfortably, a mug of hot chocolate in her hands, did she let her speak.

"The girl's had a shock," she snorted. "The most important thing is to look after her. Everything else can wait."

Jessie smiled at her gratefully and took a sip

of chocolate. It was deliciously warm and sweet. Already she was feeling much better.

"I really am all right now, Maybelle," she said softly. "I'll tell you what happened. Then maybe we can work out what it all means."

Slowly and clearly, Jessie told them the story of finding Valda at the Bins' house. She told them what Valda had said to her. And what had happened then.

As she spoke, she saw Patrice's eyes grow wider and wider, and Giff look more and more surprised. But Maybelle frowned, deep in thought.

"I don't understand this at all," she huffed, when Jessie had finished. "It must have taken a huge amount of Valda's magic to break into the human world. Why would she do it? What's the point?"

Jessie licked her lips. She'd wondered about that, too. And she'd had an idea. A horrible one. She could hardly bear to put it into words.

"Maybe Valda's realized that she really can't get back into the Realm," she said. "So she's decided to try to rule the human world instead. With her ogres and trolls and horrible monsters—"

She broke off. Patrice, Maybelle, and Giff were shaking their heads.

"That would be impossible, Jessie," said Patrice. "Valda can live in the human world, because she's one of the Folk. Like your grandmother, Queen Jessica."

"But none of the other Realm creatures can live there forever," Maybelle added. "They can only visit for a short time. If the ogres and trolls stayed in your world, they'd fade away. Valda couldn't use them to help her for very long."

"Yes. The Realm is what Valda wants," said Patrice firmly. "We can be sure of that. Don't forget, I've known her since she was a baby, just like I've known Helena and Jessica. I know all about her. It's what she's always wanted—to rule the Realm."

She shook her head. "Even after she was banished to the Outlands she never gave up. She just became more and more wicked, and more and more determined. She and her creatures have tried to invade us before, and now they're trying again."

Giff whimpered in fright.

"But there's something else we can be sure of," said Maybelle. "Whatever Valda's doing in your world, Jessie, it's all part of her plan. She never does anything without a reason."

Jessie sipped her chocolate. Her head felt much clearer now.

Valda never does anything without a reason, she thought. So what has she done up till now? She's got herself into the human world. She's made friends with the Bins family. She's got Granny and Mum out of the way. And she's done all that because . . . because . . .

Suddenly, with a chill, she understood. She put down her cup.

"Valda knows she can't get through the hedge," she said. "She can't break the Realm magic. She's tried and tried, and she can't do it. So she's thought of another way. She's going to try to get into the Realm through the human world. Through the

Door in the Blue Moon garden."

The others gaped at her. "But that's impossible!" exclaimed Patrice. "For a start, the Door won't open for her. She's too wicked. The Door won't open for evil people or creatures."

Jessie bit her lip. "Valda knows I use the Door," she said, trying to stop her voice from trembling. "I think she's going to try to make me take her through. And all her trolls and ogres as well!"

"But she couldn't make you!" exclaimed Giff. "You'd have to agree. And you wouldn't do it! You wouldn't betray us to Valda and the Outlanders, Jessie, would you?"

"Of course she wouldn't," snapped Maybelle, lashing her tail furiously. "Not if she could help it. But Valda probably has a plan to deal with that, too. I think Jessie's right. Valda is going to try to force her into opening the Door."

"Well, Queen Helena will just lock it," cried Patrice. "We'll go to her now and tell her— Oh!" Her face went pale.

"Exactly," said Maybelle grimly. "Queen

Helena isn't here. She's far away, in the west, with almost all the guards. Looking into the so-called 'trouble' there."

"You mean the trolls aren't *really* trying to break down the hedge in the west?" quavered Giff. "You mean it was a trick?"

"Yes, I think so," said Jessie. "I think Valda left a small group of trolls there, to make a lot of noise, so people would think they were planning something. The idea was to make Queen Helena go far away from here. So she wouldn't be around to lock the Door. And it worked."

"Then Queen Jessica will have to lock it, from her side," Patrice exclaimed. "Queen Jessica can face Valda, and protect Jessie, and— Oh!" She broke off again.

"Yes," said Jessie wearily. "Granny's not at Blue Moon. She's at the hospital. The phone won't work. And the roads are choked by snow. No cars can drive on them."

"This is awful!" wailed Giff.

Jessie nodded. It was all quite clear to her now.

"Valda planned it all," she said. "She waited for just the right time. She knew it would snow some time this winter. And as soon as she knew the snow was coming, she put her plan into action."

Maybelle, Patrice, and Giff glanced at one another. Patrice took Giff's hand.

"Valda even got my mother out of the way so I'd be quite alone," Jessie went on quietly. "And she made friends with the people next door, so she could wait in their house and keep an eye on me."

"The cunning, wicked . . . " Patrice's cheeks weren't pale any longer. They were red with rage.

"Well, we'll show her!" shrieked Giff. "Jessie can stay here with us. Till the snow melts, and Queen Jessica comes back to Blue Moon, and Queen Helena comes back here."

Swallowing hard, Jessie shook her head. "I can't stay here," she whispered. "I have to go back, before this afternoon."

"But why?" demanded Patrice, wide-eyed.

"Valda—she threatened me," Jessie said in a low voice. "She said that if I didn't agree to take her into the Blue Moon garden she'd let her ogres and trolls and goblins loose at the concert."

"She said *that* in front of your next-door neighbors?" Giff gasped.

Jessie shook her head. "She didn't want Mr. Bins and Irena to understand, so she didn't say it clearly. But I knew what she meant."

She shivered as she remembered Valda's words: *All your little school friends are singing in the choir at the concert, aren't they? So sweet. I have a group of friends just nearby. . . . I'm sure my friends would love to meet the choir.*

"That wicked woman's thought of everything!" Patrice moaned. "If Jessie stays here, her friends are in danger. If she goes back, *we're* in danger. What in the Realm are we going to do?"

"We're doomed!" wailed Giff. "Doomed!"

"Be quiet!" ordered Maybelle. She pawed the ground, her head hanging low.

Jessie was worried and frightened, too. And she hated seeing her friends like this. My friends in the Realm, and my friends in my own world, she thought. *Valda's threatening them both. And using me to do it. How dare she?*

"Listen," she said angrily. "We don't have to give up. There's another way. We can fight."

Maybelle shook her head. "That's impossible, Jessie," she said. "Most of the guards are far away. And once Valda and her army come through the Door—"

"No!" Jessie broke in. "I don't mean fight Valda here. I mean fight her *there*, in my world. Drive her back to where she came from."

She looked around eagerly. "I could do it," she urged. "Or at least I could try. I just need to take her by surprise. And I need something to help me. Something, anything, that Valda is afraid of."

"Valda's not afraid of anything," said Maybelle. "Except Queen Jessica, maybe."

"There must be something else," Jessie insisted. She grabbed Patrice's hand. "Come on, Patrice! You knew Valda when she was little. You're more likely than anyone to know. Think!"

Patrice stared blankly ahead. For a few long

moments there was silence. Then, suddenly, her face lit up.

"There *is* something . . . " she began. But then her eyes dulled again and she shook her head. "No, that's no use," she muttered. "Silly of me."

"Patrice, what is it?" demanded Jessie. "Is it something that scares Valda?"

"Oh yes, dearie." Patrice nodded slowly. "Scares her to death. Always has. But —"

Jessie clapped her hands. "Well, then, it's perfect!" she shouted. She jumped up. "Patrice! Tell us! What is it?"

Patrice glanced at Maybelle and at Giff. Then she looked back at Jessie. "It's no use, you know, Jessie," she said. "But if you insist, I'll tell you." She took a deep breath. "Valda's terrified of unicorns."

CHAPTER SEVEN

The forest of dreams

"Unicorns? Well, where can we find some?" Jessie asked urgently.

There was silence.

Jessie looked around. "What's the matter?" she demanded.

Maybelle was staring at the ground, frowning. Giff was looking terrified. Patrice's rosy face was sorrowful.

"You don't understand, dearie," Patrice said softly. "Unicorns are . . . special."

Giff clasped his hands. The tips of his ears were pink. "We couldn't ask the unicorns to help," he whispered.

Maybelle stood silent. Jessie turned to her. "Maybelle?" she begged. "What's the problem?"

Slowly the little horse raised her head. And Jessie was astonished to see that her usual bossy, proud look was entirely gone. Her eyes were soft and shining.

"I'll try to explain it to you, Jessie," she said quietly. "Unicorns are very wise and very powerful. They live in the Realm, but they are not like its ordinary creatures. They keep to themselves. They don't interfere."

"But the Realm is in danger!" Jessie exclaimed. "And if unicorns are the only thing Valda is afraid of, they're the only thing that can help us! Where do they live?"

"In the Forest of Dreams," murmured Maybelle.

"Would it take us long to get there?" cried Jessie.

Maybelle shook her head. "Oh no," she said. "It's very near. In one way."

"Then let's do it! Let's go now!" Jessie cried.

Patrice smoothed her apron with trembling

hands. "Listen, dearie," she said. "Put the unicorns out of your mind. It was silly of me to mention them. The unicorns won't help us. They won't go into the human world."

"Not anymore," Maybelle added gruffly. "There was a time when they did, now and then. When they felt at home there. But now they stay in the Forest of Dreams. And they never leave it. They don't welcome visitors."

Jessie looked at her friends in despair. Then she remembered something. A painting, hanging in the kitchen at Blue Moon.

It was one of her grandfather's pictures of the Realm. One of Granny's favorites. There were many trees, with tiny pale green leaves and slim white trunks. Between the trees walked a beautiful woman with long red hair. Beside her, head bent to nuzzle at her shoulder, was a magnificent white unicorn with a golden horn. Beneath its shining hoofs, flowers sprang from the grass.

Jessie knew that the woman was Granny when she was young. When she was Princess Jessica of the Realm. When she and Helena and their cousin

Valda lived in the palace together.

"Granny knew the unicorns," she said. "She visited them."

"Yes, she did, dearie," Patrice admitted. "And her sister Helena, too. Even then the unicorns kept to themselves. But they always welcomed the little princesses."

"Then perhaps they'll welcome me, too," said Jessie. "Or at least listen to what I have to say." She spun around to face Maybelle. "Oh, please let's try, Maybelle. We have to try. Please!"

Maybelle sighed. "All right," she said. "We'll try."

Jessie changed back into her own clothes, now dry and warm again. Then the four friends left the palace and began walking, with Maybelle in the lead.

Jessie had been expecting to go somewhere she'd never been before. She was surprised when the little horse led them first through the grove of pale-leaved trees, then along the road toward the Door.

"Where are we going?" she asked.

"I told you. To the Forest of Dreams," said Maybelle. But she didn't say it impatiently. She plodded along, looking neither to the right nor left, her eyes dark and serious.

Jessie could see that Maybelle wasn't going to say any more. So she turned to Patrice, who was trotting along beside her, with the frightened Giff clutching her arm.

"Patrice, tell me why Valda is afraid of the unicorns," she said. "The unicorn in my grandfather's painting looks so beautiful. And so loving."

"Unicorns can feel a generous heart," said Patrice. "Goodness warms them, like the sun. That's why they loved Jessica. And Helena, as well. But they can feel wickedness, too. It's cold, like snow."

She shrugged her plump shoulders. "Even as a child Valda had a sly way about her. She pretended to be sweetness itself. But she was cruel to any creature smaller and weaker than herself."

She sighed. "She only visited the Forest of Dreams once. With Jessica and Helena. And the unicorns attacked her, and drove her away. They knew her, you see. They could see straight through her beauty, and her fine clothes, to the cold heart inside. She was terrified. And afterward she was very ill. For months she had no strength at all."

"They hurt her so badly?" Jessie gasped. It was hard for her to believe that the splendid, gentle creature of her grandfather's painting could be savage.

"She only had one mark on her," said Patrice. "A little red mark like a tiny burn, on her shoulder blade. The point of a horn had just touched her as she turned to run. But that one touch did all the damage. And ever afterward she was scared to death of the unicorns. She shook all over if anyone even mentioned them."

They passed the place where Jessie knew the invisible Door would open, if she so wished. She shivered. Beyond it a white, cold world was waiting for her. And Valda.

Then, by the side of the road a little way ahead, she saw something she'd never noticed before. The glimmer of slim white trunks. And, above them, leaves like a green mist, trembling in the warm breeze. She stopped and pointed, too astonished to speak.

"Yes. The Forest of Dreams," said Maybelle.

"But . . . it wasn't there before," stammered Jessie. "I've looked up this way lots of times. And I've never noticed it."

"You only see the Forest of Dreams if you're looking for it, Jessie," Patrice said softly.

They moved on. Jessie kept her eyes fixed on the trees. She kept thinking they might disappear again. She could hear the beating of her heart. A feeling was growing inside her. A feeling of wonder, shyness, and fear.

"I'm scared, Patrice," she heard Giff breathe, behind her.

"You don't have to be scared," Patrice said. "Giff, believe me. The unicorns won't hurt you."

"But I've done so many bad things," whimpered Giff. "I've broken things, and I've been selfish, and made mistakes, and . . . "

"You've got a good heart, Giff. You care about other people. That's the important thing. Don't worry. You'll be quite safe."

The white-trunked trees were right beside them now. The leaves rustled in a misty cloud of green above their heads.

"Stay together," muttered Maybelle. She lowered her head and stepped off the road. Jessie followed, with Giff and Patrice close behind.

Very quickly the trunks seemed to close in around them. The fluttering leaves formed a roof over their heads. At their feet there were flowers. The golden air was sweet and warm.

Jessie glanced behind her. She could no longer see the road. Her heart beat faster. She put her hand on Maybelle's shoulder. The tiny horse looked up at her, but didn't stop walking.

"Be ready, Jessie," she said. Her voice trembled. She wasn't frightened, exactly. Jessie could see that. She was nervous, and very excited. As though she was about to meet someone very, very important.

For the first time, Jessie had a pang of doubt. Should she have insisted on coming here?

She felt Maybelle's shoulder twitch and heard her take a sudden deep breath. She looked up.

There was an open space ahead. A place of soft grass, flowers, and sunlight. The trees made a ring around it. A crystal clear pool lay like a round mirror in the center. And standing, lying on the grass, drinking from the pool, their horns flashing in the sun, were the most magnificent creatures Jessie had ever seen.

The unicorns.

CHAPTER EIGHT

The unicorn

The largest of the unicorns moved forward, stepping gracefully over the fine grass.

He stopped right in front of Jessie, raised his head, and gazed at her. His eyes, fixed on hers, were as blue as the sky.

Jessie felt a tingle run through her from her toes to the top of her head. It was as though those eyes were seeing right into her mind. To her innermost thoughts. To her memories.

She wanted to look away, but she couldn't. She just stood, one hand on Maybelle's bowed head, the other pressed to her heart.

The moment seemed endless. Jessie could hear Giff panting with fear and the soft whispering of the forest leaves. But her whole world had shrunk to two pools of blue. She felt as though she were being drawn into them. Drowning in them.

And then the eyes changed. They darkened and warmed. And Jessie felt a glow, a feeling of welcome and peace, flooding over her. She heard herself sigh.

The unicorn nodded, as if satisfied. Then he waited. No one said a word. But Jessie knew that she had passed some sort of test. Now she had to speak—to explain why she had come to the forest, and what she wanted.

It was hard to find the words. The human world, and Valda, and the terrible danger she and her friends were facing, suddenly seemed very far away.

At last she understood how Patrice and Maybelle had felt about asking the unicorns to help. It seemed impossible that any one of them would agree to leave this perfect place and go with her.

And then she remembered her grandfather's

painting. The unicorn nuzzling at her grand-mother's shoulder, full of love and happiness.

She found her voice at last. "Please," she said. "Can you help us?"

The unicorn stared at her silently. Behind him, in the clearing, the other unicorns stirred. They were listening, too.

Not all of them were white with golden horns. Some were gray, or red-brown, or black. Some had white horns, or brown ones. Some, maybe the younger ones, had no horns at all. They looked like ordinary horses. But they were the sleekest, healthiest, noblest horses Jessie had ever seen.

The unicorn was waiting for her to speak. Jessie tried to collect her thoughts. She wondered where to begin. With her grandmother? Or the Door? Or the snow? Or Valda's plan? Or . . . ?

Then she looked again into those wise blue eyes. And suddenly she realized that she didn't have to explain anything. The unicorn knew it all. He had seen it when he looked into her mind and heart.

"Will . . . will you come with me?" she stammered. "Through the Door? Into my world?

Will you help me?"

The unicorn didn't move.

"If you don't, I don't know what I'll do!" Jessie cried. "I'll have to decide—between my world and the Realm. And I can't do it! I can't!"

The unicorn turned his head and looked back at his family and friends gathered by the pool. And Jessie felt his thoughts.

"Yes. You will all be safe here, whatever happens," she said. "I understand that now. You can defend the Forest of Dreams. Valda and the Outlanders wouldn't dare to touch you or harm you. But . . . but they can hurt everyone and everything else."

Still the unicorn stood motionless.

Jessie felt Maybelle twitch nervously beneath her hand. A terrible pain gripped her heart at the thought of the little horse's fear.

"They'll take Maybelle, and all her friends, to work in their mines, away from the light and air." She choked. "How could you let that happen? They're little, but they're your cousins, all the same. And they think you're wonderful."

The unicorn gazed at her, unmoved, unblinking.

Jessie couldn't bear it. She clenched her fists. Her voice rose. "But *I* don't think you're so wonderful!" she burst out. "What good is it, being noble and wise and powerful, if you just live for yourselves and won't help anyone else?"

"Jessie!" warned Patrice quickly.

Jessie stopped, panting. She realized she'd been almost shouting. She'd lost her temper. She felt herself blushing with shame. Now the unicorn would be angry. She'd ruined everything.

"I'm sorry," she whispered. Tears brimmed in her eyes. She turned away.

Through her tears she saw Patrice and Giff staring wide-eyed at her. Then she heard a tiny sound. And felt a warm, silky touch on her shoulder.

She realized that it was the unicorn. He had moved very close to her and was nuzzling at her, his blue eyes full of understanding and friendship.

You are very like your grandmother, Jessie. Full of life, and love. And you are right. Perhaps we have kept to ourselves for too long. I will go with you.

Jessie felt the words, and the warm glow that

came with them. She saw Maybelle lift her head and gaze at the unicorn with shining eyes, as he went back to the pool to farewell his watching friends. She heard Patrice and Giff whispering, astounded, behind her.

And then the unicorn was back, leading the way out of the forest, toward the Door. And flowers were springing from the ground wherever he trod.

They reached the Door. Jessie pressed her lips together. She knew they couldn't delay. Soon the Bins family would be leaving for the concert. If she was late . . .

"It's very cold on the other side," she murmured to the unicorn. "And I think Valda will be waiting."

He nodded.

Patrice, Maybelle, and Giff had been talking together.

"Jessie, we want to go with you," Maybelle said firmly. "We've decided. We can't let you do this alone."

Patrice nodded, and Giff, trembling all over, nodded, too.

She is not alone, little cousin.

They all felt the words. The unicorn raised his head proudly.

It does you and your friends credit that you wish to help. But it would be foolish for you to come with us. You cannot stand against Valda. Her wickedness has grown strong, in the Outlands. She could take one or all of you into her power, and threaten you. That way she could force Jessie to do her will. And then the cause would be lost. Do you understand?

They did. Jessie could see it. And the unicorn's words reminded her, too, of the terrible danger she was about to face.

She hugged her friends, one by one. "Wait for us," she murmured.

Think strong thoughts for us. The unicorn bent his head, touching first Giff, then Patrice, then Maybelle with his shining golden horn. Then he turned to Jessie and waited.

She put one hand on his shoulder. "Open!" she called. And, with a rush and a swirl of icy air, they moved through the Door.

CHAPTER NINE

A Terrible Choice

Jessie opened her eyes. In the secret garden everything gleamed white. Through the doorway in the hedge she could see the house and the huge trees that stood in front of it, their dark branches loaded with snow.

There was a breathless hush. A few last snowflakes drifted from gray skies. There was no sign of Valda.

The unicorn stood motionless behind her. She glanced at him. His spotless white coat matched the snow so completely that he was almost invisible except for his horn and his eyes. But Jessie could feel his warmth against her back, and it comforted her.

In the distance, from the Bins' house, she heard Irena calling to her father. She sounded angry. Her father called something in reply. They hadn't left for the concert yet, then. But Valda wasn't here, waiting, as Jessie had expected she'd be.

Hope fluttered in her heart. Was it possible that Valda had gone away? Given up?

No. She is here. Very near. I feel her. Be ready.

The words, deep with warning, sounded in her mind. She jerked around to face the secret garden entrance again. And as she did there was a squeak of snow under a boot and a swirl of purple, and Valda stepped into the doorway, laughing in triumph. She had been waiting, all along, hidden behind the hedge.

"So, Jessie," she began, spreading her arms to block the doorway. "You have decided to come to your senses. You have returned. I knew you would. And now, now you will open the Door for me, you stupid little — "

The unicorn pushed past Jessie, his eyes cold blue fire. The snow hissed and crackled under his feet, melting and then freezing again into tiny, flashing pebbles of ice as he passed.

Valda broke off with a hiss and staggered backward. Her hands, tipped with long red fingernails, jabbed at the air.

"Keep back!" she screeched. "Keep back!"

The unicorn walked on, taking his time. His golden horn gleamed. He took Valda's place in the doorway of the secret garden, almost filling it with his great body.

Behind him stood Jessie, shivering and terrified, but protected. Outside, under the great bare trees, Valda raged, scratching at the air.

Return to the Outlands where you belong, Valda. You cannot have the Realm. Or any of the creatures in it. You cannot harm this world. Or you will answer to me.

Jessie clasped her hands as the unicorn's unspoken words thrilled through her.

There was a moment's terrifying silence. It was as though the whole Blue Moon garden was holding its breath. Then . . .

"Hello! Miss Outlander! Are you there?" Mr. Bins' voice sounded thin and a little cross as it floated down to them from the side of the house.

Oh no! thought Jessie.

"There she is!" shouted Irena. "Down at the bottom of the yard. Maybe she saw something! Go and ask her, Dad. Go on!"

Jessie heard Valda laugh. It was a chilling sound. She knew what it meant.

"What is it, Mr. Bins?" called Valda. "Come closer. I can't quite hear you."

Jessie ran to the unicorn's side and stood on tiptoes to peer over his shoulder. She saw Mr. Bins, plump and fussy, picking his way through the snow toward Valda. Irena was stumbling after him.

"I've been looking for you, Miss Outlander," Mr. Bins was panting. "Aren't you coming with us to the Winter Festival? We'll have to walk to the town hall, I'm afraid, because the roads are blocked with snow. So we really must be leaving. I mustn't be late for my speech, you know."

"Dad! Don't worry about all that stuff! Ask her about Grey Prince," screeched Irena. "She might have seen which way he went. Ask her!"

"Come here, Irena dear," called Valda, stretching out her hand. "Tell me all about it."

"Mr. Bins! Irena!" Jessie screamed, as loudly as she could. "Stay away from her! Don't go near her!"

Mr. Bins stopped, very startled, and looked around. He couldn't see anything but Valda, snow and trees.

"Is Jessie here?" he asked.

"She's playing silly games, I'm afraid. Hide-and-seek." Valda's red lips curved into a smile. Her red-tipped fingers beckoned. "Come closer, Mr. Bins."

"No, Mr. Bins!" shouted Jessie. She struggled to get past the unicorn, but he stood firm.

Stay in safety, Jessie.

"I can't." She gasped. "I've got to stop them. Warn them. Valda—she's going to—"

"Where is that rat Jessie?" shrilled Irena. She was scarlet with rage. "I can hear her but I can't

91

see her!" she stormed. "Where is she, Miss Outlander? Boy, am I going to get her. My stupid
horse broke down its stupid fence and ran away.
And it's all her crazy grandmother's fault. She's the
one who upset him in the first place. I'm going to
get the whole crazy family put in jail, that's what
I'm going to do!"

She overtook her father and rushed, slipping
and sliding, toward Valda. Valda reached out and
grabbed her, laughing.

And then Irena screamed.

"Wha—what's the matter, Irena?" stuttered
Mr. Bins, breaking into a run.

Valda laughed, and snatched at his arm, too.
Horrified, Jessie saw the confusion, fear, and pain
on his face as her icy grip tightened.

Valda whirled to face Jessie and the unicorn,
dragging her prisoners with her. She wasn't smiling now. She was scowling fiercely. "Now!" she
snarled. "Now we will see."

Jessie saw Mr. Bins' and Irena's faces grow
pale with shock. Their mouths hung open as they

stared at the unicorn. His golden horn gleamed. His eyes shone with blue fire. Glittering crystals of ice tumbled beneath his stamping hoofs.

Irena shrieked. Valda's fingers tightened spitefully around her arm. "Be quiet, you little fool!" she said.

Then she flung back her head. "Gather together, my creatures!" she shouted. "Be ready! Soon I will call you to join me. Soon the Door will be open. The Realm will be yours. As I promised."

A hideous low muttering, a cackling and grunting, rose and echoed all around them. Monstrous shapes began wavering in the frosty air.

Irena covered her eyes and sobbed. Mr. Bins stared around him wildly.

The unicorn stepped forward. Jessie moved with him, her hand on his shoulder. She could feel the great muscles moving under his skin. She felt the words beaming out of him with enormous power.

Back, evil ones!

The shapes faded. The muttering faltered, and died away.

Valda bared her teeth. "Tell your friend the unicorn to stand aside, Jessie," she growled. "Tell him not to interfere with me. Or you will see these miserable neighbors of yours thrown into the Outlands. My hungriest soldiers are waiting for them there. They will not survive for long. See? They are helpless."

She shook Irena and Mr. Bins like rag dolls.

"Leave them alone!" screamed Jessie. She didn't like Mr. Bins. She didn't like Irena. But she couldn't bear seeing *anyone* hurt and terrified like this. It was too awful.

Valda smiled. "What happens to them is up to you." She purred. "Say the word, and they are free." She paused. "Well, Jessie? Are you going to save them, or not?"

CHAPTER TEN

Rescue

"Jessie," whimpered Irena. Her face was streaked with tears, her teeth were chattering with terror. "What's happening? Are we dreaming? Oh, say we're dreaming!"

Jessie couldn't answer. How could she even begin to explain?

"Jessie, help us!" sobbed Irena. "Please! I'm sorry I was mean to you! I'm sorry!"

The unicorn raised his head.

It was by your will that I came here, Jessie. I will obey your wish. What do you wish, Jessie?

"I wish Granny was here!" Jessie cried aloud.

Mr. Bins struggled in Valda's iron grip. "Jessie," he moaned. "For goodness' sake, what on earth could your grandmother do about anything? If this—this person wants something from you, do it! Do it!" His eyes popping, he stared at the unicorn as though he thought he was going mad.

"You heard the man, Jessie!" shouted Valda. "Do as he says. Let me through the Door. And my creatures with me. What does it matter to you?"

She raised her voice to a ringing cry. "The Realm is not your world, Jessie. It wasn't even good enough for your precious grandmother. She left it, didn't she, in her time? Now it's your turn."

"No it isn't!"

The shout came from the top of the garden. It came with a thunder of flying hoofs, a streak of orange fur, the scattering of snow.

Grey Prince came galloping through the trees, his eyes wide and bright. Sweat frothed on his gray coat. Beside him raced Flynn. And on his back was a proud figure with a long gray plait, pink cheeks, and a face filled with fury.

"Granny!" squealed Jessie. So Flynn had managed to bring Granny home after all! He had done it by calling on Grey Prince to help. Of course! A horse could make its way through the snow, even if a car couldn't.

She clutched at the unicorn's mane. He stared at Granny, and bowed to the ground.

Granny sprang from Grey Prince's back and faced Valda. Valda cringed away from her, throwing Mr. Bins and Irena aside. They sprawled on the snow and lay still. But Granny looked only at Valda.

"Again you have tried to take the Realm, Valda!" she shouted. "And this time you have dared to do it by using my granddaughter."

She lifted her hand, her face stern.

Valda drew herself up and stared at the old woman. "Do your worst, Queen Jessica," she sneered. "I do not fear you. You will not kill me. I know that. You will send me back to the Outlands. And there I will grow stronger and stronger with every year that passes."

Her mouth twisted as she jeered. "You live in the human world, Queen Jessica. Already you are wrinkled and your hair is white. You are old. One day you will die. And then—then I will come back. And nothing will stop me. Nothing! No weak child, or ugly unicorn, or sneaking cat—or broken-down old horse!"

She lashed out at Grey Prince, hitting his soft nose with her hand. He jerked and whinnied in pain.

Valda laughed.

And then Jessie felt the unicorn move. He lunged forward, faster than she could ever have imagined. And his golden horn just touched Valda's hand. The hand with which she had beaten Grey Prince.

There was a moment's absolute silence. Then there was a shriek of rage and a flash of light—and then, suddenly, Valda disappeared. Nothing remained in her place but a small pile of gray ash lying on the snow.

Mr. Bins and Irena leaped to their feet. They both looked at the pile of ash. They looked at Granny, at Jessie, at the unicorn, its eyes burning blue.

And then they ran, screaming, from the Blue Moon garden.

The Bins family moved away, after that. They had to, really. They were too embarrassed to stay.

Everyone at school told Jessie how Mr. Bins and Irena had staggered into the town hall, right in the middle of the Winter Festival concert.

They'd burst in through the doors, raving about unicorns and monsters and witches. People tried to quiet them, but they just kept babbling that someone had exploded into ash before their eyes, and that old Mrs. Jessica Belairs was some sort of fairy queen.

"No one believed them, of course," Jessie giggled as she ate cakes and drank bubbling pink lemonade in Patrice's kitchen just a week afterward. "Everyone thought they were just out of their minds, or had had some sort of weird dream. No one else but them had seen Valda, anyway. And who'd believe that Granny was a queen?"

"Who indeed?" Granny laughed from her end of the table.

"I would," said Giff shyly.

"So would I," agreed Maybelle, shaking her mane so that the ribbons flew.

"She's never been anything else to me," said Patrice quietly.

"Or me," Queen Helena smiled.

Jessie looked at Granny. She certainly looked like a fairy queen at this moment. Beautiful and very happy. As always, when the magic of the Realm worked on her, her long hair was shining golden red. In the Realm Granny looked as young as Helena. But her sparkling green eyes were unchanged.

To Jessie, she was still Granny. And at home, gray hair or not, she was still beautiful.

"I must say, I don't think I'll miss the Bins family very much," Granny was telling Helena now. "And you know what? I don't think they'll miss us, either."

Everyone laughed. Giff took the opportunity to help himself to another cake.

Jessie looked around. She sighed with happiness.

"Yes," said Queen Helena, as if she was feeling Jessie's thoughts. "The Realm was nearly lost. But now it is safe. Thanks to you, Jessie."

She turned to her sister. "And to you, Jessica."

Granny smiled. "I did very little," she said. "And I wouldn't have been able to do anything if it hadn't been for Flynn, and Grey Prince, and the unicorn."

Her face grew serious for a moment. "Valda was right. I would never have been able to make myself destroy her. So she would have been a menace to the Realm forever. But the unicorn . . . "

Giff shivered.

"The unicorn just touched her," whispered Jessie. "That was all he did. But . . . " Her voice trailed away. She still didn't quite understand what had happened to Valda.

"The unicorn's touch destroys all that is wicked," Helena told her gently. "That's why, I think, Valda was so sick and weak after she first visited the Forest of Dreams when we were children. Even then, she had a bad streak. So the unicorn's touch burned and weakened her."

"But the Valda we met at Blue Moon was all bad, Jessie," said Granny. "There must have been no good left in her at all. And so, when the unicorn touched her, she just—disappeared."

"He did it when he saw her hit Grey Prince," said Jessie, remembering. "He couldn't stand it. Poor Grey Prince."

Maybelle grinned. "You don't have to be sorry for Grey Prince anymore, Jessie," she said. "There's not a more contented horse in the Realm. I saw him yesterday. Sleek, and happy, and feeling wonderful—in the Forest of Dreams."

"Yes." Granny smiled. "I'm so glad the unicorn took him home. Of course, it's been done before. Unicorns often adopted stray horses in the old days. There are quite a few already in the Forest of Dreams. I knew Grey Prince would feel at home there."

She sighed happily, and sipped her lemonade. "I paid Irena for him, of course. She left town without ever knowing what happened to him. She didn't care, anyway."

"More cake, anyone?" asked Patrice.

Giff nodded eagerly, and she frowned at him.

Jessie laughed. She reached out for another cake herself, and her charm bracelet jingled on her wrist. She looked at it.

So many charms. Every one told the story of an adventure. And now she had a new one, set with a shining crystal.

"Ice made by unicorns' hoofs never melts, Jessie," Queen Helena had told her, giving her the charm. "So here is an ice-crystal for you to wear on your bracelet. Now you'll never forget."

Jessie looked at the charm and remembered the unicorn's soft touch of farewell. And his unspoken words.

Come and see me again, Jessie. Do not forget me. Come and see us all again. In the Forest of Dreams.

"I will," she whispered to herself. "I'll never forget." She touched the tiny gold-and-crystal charm, and all the other charms dangling from her wrist. She smiled.

She knew that she didn't need a charm to

remember this particular adventure. As long as she lived, she'd remember the day she met the unicorn, the day they defeated Valda, and the day Grey Prince found a family and a home.

Because that was the day that she, and her very special grandmother, made sure that their friends in the wonderful world of the Realm really would live happily ever after.